MOLLIE HUNTER

The Smartest Man in Ireland

Patrick Kentigern Keenan called himself
the smartest man in Ireland and it was his
greatest wish to outwit the cunning
fairies. So on the night he came upon the
beautiful fairy horses and their riders, he
was determined to capture one of their
magical beasts for himself.

But the fairy horse proved more than
Patrick had bargained for and soon he
found himself on a wild moonlit chase
across the countryside . . .

THE
SMARTEST
MAN
IN IRELAND

Mollie Hunter

Illustrated by Charles Keeping

A Magnet Book

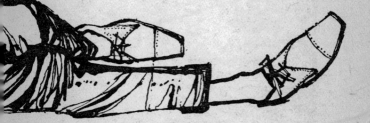

First published 1963
by Blackie & Son Limited
This Magnet edition published 1986
by Methuen Children's Books Ltd
11 New Fetter Lane, London EC4P 4EE
Text copyright © 1963 Maureen Mollie Hunter McIlwraith
Illustrations copyright © 1963 Blackie & Son Ltd
Printed in Great Britain
by Richard Clay (The Chaucer Press) Ltd,
Bungay, Suffolk

ISBN 0 416 52890 2

to MICHAEL, *with love*

Contents

The Smartest Man in Ireland

1
The
New
Shoes

There was a man once lived in Connemara and his name was Patrick Kentigern Keenan. Every bone in his body was lazy and he never did a stroke of work if he could help it, but all the same, he had a great opinion of himself.

"I'm the smartest man in Ireland," he used to say.

He was a man that was greatly troubled with curiosity, this Patrick. Moreover, he was very fond of good dress, and so there was nothing he liked better than roaming about the countryside, dressed like a lord and poking his long nose into things that were no concern of his.

The folk of Connemara shook their heads over Patrick Kentigern Keenan and told him, "You'll come to a bad end, so you will." But Patrick only laughed at them. "I'll live to surprise the lot of ye," he said, "for I'm the smartest man in Ireland." A terrible boaster, he was.

Now this Patrick had a wife called Bridget and she, poor soul, had a hard time of it, never knowing when the pig would die on her for lack of meal or the bailiff turn her out for the rent not being paid. Still, she was a good wife to Patrick and wouldn't hear a word against him, though she wasn't above giving him the rough edge of her own tongue when his idle ways and foolish talk got beyond bearing.

All in all though, they got along well enough together for they had a great affection for one another and their baby son Kieron was the joy of their lives. And so they might have gone on without any great upset to the end of their natural lives if Patrick hadn't decided one day that he would like to have a pair of new shoes.

As soon as the idea came into his head, nothing would please him but that they must be made by the leprechauns for, as everybody knows, they are the finest shoemakers in Ireland. But leprechauns have to be paid in gold for their work, and it's a brave man that will try and cheat them. All the same, Patrick made up his mind to do just that, and that was the beginning of all his trouble.

He waited till Bridget was out visiting a neighbor one day, and then he went and took the shilling that she had hidden in the china jug on the mantelshelf and painted it over with gold paint. The dear knows where he got the gold paint but you can be sure he didn't buy it!

That night he went out and laid the false gold on the stump of a tree beside a thorn bush that folk called The Fairies' Thorn—and no shame in him either, for as he went home he laughed and said to himself, "Tomorrow night I'll have the finest shoes in Ireland."

Sure enough, when he went back to the tree stump the next night, the money was gone and there were a pair of new shoes lying in its place. They were a grand pair of shoes, polished and shining, made of the softest of leather, and with stitches so small and fine you could hardly see them. Patrick put them on, and they fitted like a glove.

He sat down on the tree stump and stretched out his feet to

admire them. "There's no doubt about it," he said, "I'm the smartest man in Ireland." And he ran all the way home to show Bridget the new shoes. But when he got home, there was Bridget sitting in her chair by the fire holding her apron up to her eyes and she was wailing and lamenting.

"Oh, Patrick!" she cried when she saw him. "The baby's gone from his cradle and there's a leprechaun in his place. A nasty little old man in the cradle and my little Kieron gone. Oh! Oh! Oh!" Bridget sobbed, and the tears ran down her cheeks like rain.

"Have your senses left ye entirely, woman!" roared Patrick. He dashed forward and looked in the cradle. It was true enough. The baby was gone and there was a leprechaun there, a little man with a wrinkled brown face and a wicked grin.

"Hello, Patrick," he said cheerfully. "And how d'ye like the fit of your new shoes?"

At that, Patrick fell to lamenting as loud as his wife, for he saw how the leprechauns had tricked him, and the little man hopped out of the cradle and stood grinning at him.

"Cheer up, Patrick," he said. "True it is you'll never see your boy again, but you'll be happy to know that the leprechauns will bring him up to be a good shoemaker, and they'll teach him, too, to know true gold from false."

As soon as he said this, Bridget looked at Patrick's feet, and when she saw the new shoes he was wearing, she understood in a flash what had happened. It was too much even for her to put up with.

"So that was it!" she cried, jumping to her feet in a rage. "You tried to cheat the leprechauns, and now they've stolen my baby. Oh, what a fool and a bad man I have for a husband this day!" And she seized the broom and beat Patrick with it so that he ran out of the house, roaring with pain.

And that was only the beginning of the trouble. Patrick could roar and rave as much as he liked and Bridget could weep, but the leprechaun stayed on in their house. He slept all day and at night he made shoes, and as he worked, he whistled. And what with the hammering and whistling all night and Bridget weeping and blaming him for the lost baby all day, Patrick was driven nearly out of his senses. He tried every argument he knew to make the leprechaun tell him where Kieron was hidden, but the old man just grinned and whistled louder than ever. At last, he could stand it no longer and he went to the leprechaun and said:

"Now, listen, old one, I'll admit I'm not the smartest man in Ireland and that was a dirty trick I played on the leprechauns. So for the love of peace let the boy come back to us, for I haven't the life of a dog since he's gone."

The leprechaun cocked an eye at him. "It's not so easy done," he said. "You'll have to put on the shoes you stole from the leprechauns and go out and earn a gold piece for every day I've stayed in this house, and every gold piece will have to be paid over to the leprechauns."

"Well now, that's a terrible lot of money," said Patrick. "Ye're chargin' me very dear for me shoes."

"'Tisn't the regular price," said the leprechaun quickly. "It's the price a cheat pays."

"Ah well," agreed Patrick, thinking he would find some way out of it, "I'll take your bargain," and he went and put on the new shoes.

"That's settled then," said the leprechaun. "And mind, I wouldn't try to get out of the bargain if I were you. Look in the cradle now." And with that, he vanished out of their sight.

Patrick and his wife ran to look in the cradle, and Bridget wept for joy to see their son lying there as if he had never been away. As for Patrick, he sat down to admire his feet and think of a way to get out of his bargain. The next minute he let out a yell of pain, for the shoes had begun to burn his feet as if they were red hot. He tried to take the shoes off, but they stuck fast and he leapt the height of the roof with pain, while his cries were enough to bring every neighbor within a mile running to find the cause of the trouble.

"Keep your bargain, you fool!" shouted Bridget. "Have ye not brought trouble enough on us with your thievin' ways!"

"Mercy! Mercy!" yelled Patrick. "I'll keep me bargain."

He ran out of the house and seized a hoe and began hoeing the potatoes like mad, and as soon as he did this, the shoes stopped burning his feet.

"What's wrong with him at all?" asked the neighbors, all amazed, and Bridget told them how he had tried to cheat the leprechauns.

"So that's the smartest man in Ireland!" said they, and by the next fair-day the whole of Connemara was laughing at Patrick Kentigern Keenan.

The long and the short of it was that Patrick had to keep working till he had a gold piece for his labor, and then he went out and laid it on the tree stump and the next morning it was gone. This wasn't at all to his taste, and every now and then he would go back to his idle ways, but as soon as he did that, the shoes would start burning his feet and he would have to start work again. There was no way of getting out of his bargain with the leprechaun.

Bridget soon forgave him the foolish trick he had played, for with Kieron safely back in his cradle she was as happy as a lark again, and like a good soul she did her best to help Patrick earn the gold for the leprechaun, spinning and churning and weaving for the folk around from morning till night. But in spite of Bridget's help, it took him a long time to pay for his shoes, for it was true enough he had been charged very dear for them.

As time went on and he was still working hard, people began to say, "Ah, he's a hard-workin' man, is Patrick Kentigern Keenan."

Patrick liked the sound of that, for praise was meat and drink to a boastful fellow like him. In no time at all he was telling it far and wide that he was the hardest-working man in Ireland, and after a while he was adding, "and I have the finest shoes, too."

For there was a curious thing about the leprechaun's shoes. No matter what Patrick did when he wore them, they never got dirty but kept their first fine polish. No matter how long he wore them, the leather never got scratched or worn, and the tiny stitches that held them together stayed as close and neat as they had always been, so that, in the end, everyone had to agree that they were indeed the finest shoes in Ireland.

"But look at the price he paid for them," they said, and

they laughed. "Ah, there's no one smart enough to cheat the leprechauns." And nobody ever believed Patrick again when he said he was the smartest man in Ireland.

"Pay no heed to them, Patrick," Bridget said when they laughed. "They'll soon forget about the leprechaun."

However, it was all a great hurt to Patrick's pride, and he vowed that one day he would prove to the whole of Connemara that he was the smartest man in Ireland, supposing it took him the rest of his life to do it.

2
The
Golden
Crown

Once Patrick had made his vow, he felt more cheerful about
things. He was kind-hearted enough, too, in spite of his
faults, and what between that and the great conceit he had in
himself, he bore the leprechaun no ill will for getting the
better of him over the new shoes. "Sure," said he, "it's only a
matter of time and opportunity till I have the chance to show
the great and superior intelligence I have." All the same, he
couldn't help thinking that if he had every gold piece he had
paid over for the shoes collected into one purse, he would
have money enough to live like a lord.

He thought of the lost gold most of all when he took his
evening stroll along the turf track through the bog. It was a
lonely road and a sad time of day with the mist falling and
Patrick's thoughts were mournful, so the evening was all of a
piece, as you might say.

He was brooding like this one evening when he saw a man
coming toward him along the road. When he was only about

twenty yards away, Patrick said to himself, "That one's a stranger now, for I can't seem to place his face at all."

When the man was only twenty feet away, Patrick said to himself, "Well, this is a queer one. He's dressed like a man, but he's only the height of a boy." And by that time the stranger was upon him and passing the time of day.

"It's a fine evening all right, but for the mist," Patrick agreed, all the time sizing the fellow up.

He was the height of a boy of twelve, but he had the face of a man of fifty on him. His breeches were of coarse gray homespun, and he wore a short black jacket of an old-fashioned cut. His hat was black, too, with a small brim and a round crown.

"You'll be a farmer then, I suppose," Patrick said, taking this all in at a glance.

"You might call me that," said the small fellow, "seeing the great interest I take in cattle."

"Cattle, is it!" said Patrick, and you could have knocked him down with a feather, for he knew right away that he was talking to a fairy-man.

The fact is he should have known it sooner from the way the man was dressed, and him no higher than a boy, for anyone will tell you that's always how a fairy-man appears to mortal folk, but it took the mention of cattle for Patrick to put two and two together. Many a time he'd heard tell of the great herds of fairy-cattle that grazed the uplands.

For a minute he just stood there looking stupid, and then his mind began to work again. He talked of this and that with the fairy-man, and all the time he was saying to himself, "If I can think of a way to get hold of the little fellow's hat, I'm a rich man," for a fairy who loses his hat loses his magic power, and he will pay the thief anything to get it back.

"I'd like fine to get some of my cattle to market," the fairy-man said after a while, "but I haven't the time to spare and that's a fact."

"Well now, you're a lucky man to have fallen in with me," said Patrick, "for there isn't a man in Connemara, nor yet in Ireland, could drive you a better bargain."

"I don't know about that," said the fairy-man, "for I've heard tell there's a man in Connemara calls himself the smartest man in Ireland, and his name is Patrick Kentigern Keenan."

"The same!" said Patrick with a bow. "And at your service."

"Well, Mr. Keenan," said the fairy-man, returning the bow but keeping his hat on, as Patrick wasn't slow to notice, "I'll be glad to do business with you. I'll be here at sunrise tomorrow with the beasts, and I'll give you a gold piece when you take them and another two when you come back from the market."

"I couldn't have said fairer meself," said Patrick, "but when——" There was no sense in saying any more for he was talking to empty air. The fairy-man had vanished.

Wait till I get the hat off him! Patrick thought. He stuck his hands in his pockets and danced a reel by himself, laughing all the time. *That'll* prove I'm the smartest man in Ireland.

When he got home, he didn't tell Bridget a thing except that he had decided to go to the fair the next day, for he said to himself, "Sure, the woman has no sense. If she knew what I was up to, she might start layin' about me with a broom again, the way she did over the new shoes."

The next morning, Bridget put a bottle of beer and some bread and cheese into his coat pocket and Patrick set off along the road. When he came near to the place where he had met the fairy-man, he saw a great herd of cattle all moving about. As beasts go, they were on the small side, but they were fat and had a fine shine to their skins.

At the side of the road the fairy-man was lying. He still wore his gray breeches and his old-fashioned black coat, and on his head was the little, round, black hat. He seemed to be sleeping, and Patrick came quietly up behind him till the hat was within reach, and with one quick sweep of his hand he had it off the fairy-man's head.

As quick as you like, the little man jumped to his feet, and quicker than that, he was all different. The little black coat changed into a long green robe with a border of gold on it, his breeches changed suddenly to green and the belt that held them was solid gold. And instead of the face of a man of fifty, he had the face of a fair young man, and his hair was golden and streaming down his back.

Patrick staggered back with his mouth wide open. He looked at the fairy-man in front of him, and then he looked at the little black hat in his hand—only it wasn't a little black hat any longer, it was a golden crown.

The fairy-man said nothing, but his look was terrible, and Patrick would have run a mile, but his feet stuck fast to the ground with the fear on him. At last he stammered, "Y-y'r Honor, it was a j-joke. 'Deed it was. I—I wouldn't be taking the crown off a king." And he held out the golden crown to the fairy king.

At that, such a look of relief came over the fairy king's face that Patrick felt his courage coming back into his stomach again. He drew back his hand again and said boldly, "Little black hat or crown, 'tis all the same. A fairy has no magic without his hat."

"And no sense either, to trade with mortals," said the fairy king, his face as red as a turkey cock with rage, "for there's never a one yet has kept his bargain with the Good People."

"Who is it then, is breakin' a bargain?" Patrick demanded

angrily. "Takin' your cattle to market has nothing to do with takin' the hat off your head. And take your cattle to market I will, but get your crown back, you won't—not without you pay me for it."

"Take the cattle then," shouted the fairy king, "but no ransom will you get from me."

"Ah well," said Patrick, "you'll maybe come to sense before sundown. I'll off to the fair." And he tucked the crown under his arm and began to drive the beasts down the road.

They moved off slowly, making a great noise and pushing among themselves. Contrary beasts they were, and difficult to drive, but Patrick was in no hurry and sauntered along behind them, dreaming of the fine times he would have when he was a rich man. It was noon when he got to the fair, and he was hungry, but he had made up his mind to sell the cattle first and then spend the rest of the day enjoying himself.

As luck would have it, he saw a dealer that he knew, right at the edge of the ring. "Mulhoy," he shouted, and wiped his face with his sleeve. It was a hot day and the flies were buzzing round him something terrible. Mulhoy turned round and waved a hand at him.

"It's yerself, Keenan," he shouted, and began to walk toward Patrick.

The cattle were pushing and shoving back and forward, and every now and then one would give Patrick a knock that near had him on the broad of his back. And all the time, the flies got thicker and thicker round his head till he could hardly see Mulhoy through them.

"Look, man," he said to the dealer, "you'll not find the like of the cattle I have here to sell in the whole of Ireland, but I'll make a quick bargain with you or none at all, for the flies in this market have me near demented."

"Well, now, Patrick," said Mulhoy, "I'll allow the flies are the worst I've seen—they're more like a plague than a decent visitation. But sure, man, they're not botherin' me at all. It's you must have treacle in your hair to give the creatures such a love of you."

"Begob!" shouted Patrick in a fury. "Will ye shut yer trap about treacle and visitations and such, and give me a price for the cattle."

"Keenan," said Mulhoy, very quiet and dignified, "there's none of the creatures of creation between here and the ring but a cloud of flies. And I'm not in the market for flies." And he turned on his heel and walked off.

"I'll have the law on you," yelled Patrick, dancing up and down with rage and brushing flies off his face with both hands. "A hundred head of cattle, the finest in Ireland, fairy-cattle no less, and he calls them flies! He wouldn't know a cow from a pratie peel . . ." And so on.

"What's the matter with the man, at all?" the other dealers asked Mulhoy.

"Och, he's sufferin' from illusions," said Mulhoy. "He thinks he has a hundred head of fairy-cattle to sell, and what has he but a cloud of flies."

"Fairy-cattle!" said the dealers. "Now what man could come honest by the like of that? Depend upon it, he's worked the fairies an ill turn, and they've changed the cattle to flies."

They strolled across to Patrick where he danced about shouting and beating the flies away. "Is it the fairy king's crown you've stolen, then, to make the Good People take such a spite at you?" one of them shouted.

Patrick stopped his dancing as the truth suddenly struck him. "Oh, wirra, wirra!" he cried. "It is that, then." He grabbed the bulge of the crown in his pocket and took to his heels, the flies streaming after him and the laughter of the folk in his ears.

Back along the road he ran, and the faster he went, the faster the flies came after him, till he came to the place where he had met the fairy king. There, with the flies nearly smothering him, he pulled the crown from his pocket, flung it on the ground, and the flies vanished like a cloud of smoke.

Patrick sat down on the ground then, puffing like a bellows. "Not a word of this to Bridget," he said to himself. "Let the folk at the fair laugh their sides out, but I'll not be made a mock of by me own wife." And he set off for home.

"Ah, well," he said to himself as he walked, "I'll have a good meal when I get home, and that's something to be thankful for these hard times." And he began to whistle, thinking of the great plate of stirabout he would eat.

Bridget was sitting by the hearth when he came in, rocking the cradle with one foot. "I'll have me supper now, Bridget," said Patrick.

"That might be easier said than done," Bridget told him, "for there isn't a bit of meal in the house. I gave the last of it away to an old woman—hungry she was, and I couldn't refuse her."

"Well, if I haven't married the biggest fool in Connemara!" Patrick roared. "Here am I, workin' hard all day, and what do I get for me supper but the lickin' of an empty pot!"

"Ah, now, don't be angry, Patrick," Bridget coaxed him. "Such a poor old woman she was, and yet she gave the baby a present. Look, it's here in the cradle."

"What present could a beggar woman give that would be fit for my little Kieron," grumbled Patrick, peering down into the cradle.

"It was the spoon she supped the meal with," said Bridget. "She washed it and said to give it to Kieron, for it would bring him luck."

Patrick looked at the spoon, and then he picked it up for a closer look. The handle was strangely carved and set with green stones that glimmered in the dimness of the room, and the spoon itself glittered like gold.

"This beggar woman," he said to Bridget, "what was she like?"

"She was dressed in green and she was shod in green," said Bridget. "Her hair was white under a green hood, and her eyes were black."

"Bridget," said Patrick sternly, "it's easy to see you're not blessed with the great brain that I have. That old beggar woman, as you call her, dressed in green and shod in green, with her hair white and her eyes black under a green hood was the fairy queen the way she always appears to the like of us. And a golden spoon was all you got out of her for your trouble."

Bridget bent over the cradle to hide the smile that was coming on her face. "Maybe so," said she, "but as I was goin' for turf this mornin', I saw you settin' off with a great herd of cattle and a gold crown in your hand. What did *you* get for your trouble, Patrick?"

Patrick sat down then and put his head in his hands. "Bridget, Bridget," he said mournfully, "there's not a thing gone right for me this day, from the start of it to the close of it."

"Ah, well, don't break your heart over it, whatever the trouble was," Bridget said kindly, but Patrick only groaned and clutched his stomach. "If me stomach was full," he said bitterly, "me heart could take care of itself."

The smile grew on Bridget's face as she rose from her seat and picked up a covered dish that was lying on the hearth. "And did ye truly think," she asked, lifting the lid off the dish, "that I would have such a heart of stone as to let you go supperless to bed?"

"Glory be!" Patrick cried thankfully, sticking his long nose into the great cloud of savory steam that rose from the dish. "Ye've more sense than I gave ye credit for, Bridget. Where's a spoon, quick!"

"Not so fast, not so fast," said Bridget, holding the dish back. "Ye haven't told me yet what happened to the cattle you drove or the golden crown that was in your hand."

"Is tellin' you the price of me supper?" asked Patrick, quite taken aback at this but keeping his eyes fixed hard on the dish.

"It is," said Bridget firmly, holding fast to it.

Well, a hungry man is no match for a determined woman, as Patrick well knew. "Give the dish here." He sighed. "Ye might as well hear the sad tale from me as from that thievin'

rogue Mulhoy when he tells it around the country." And so Bridget handed him the dish and while he ate his supper he told her the story of the golden crown.

"I don't wonder the dealers laughed," said Bridget when he had finished. "You should take a lesson from it, Patrick. You'll never get the better of a fairy-man."

But Patrick was a different man now that he had food inside him. "Just you wait, Bridget," he said cheerfully. "The next time I meet with a fairy-man, things will turn out different. I'll prove yet that I'm the smartest man in Ireland. Just you wait and see!"

3

The
White
Hare

The day of the horse fair came round not long after this, and Patrick decided to go and see what was being offered in the way of bargains. This was natural enough for he was reckoned to be a grand judge of horseflesh, but Bridget began worrying as soon as he said he would go.

"You'll land in trouble," she said, "as sure as your name's Patrick Kentigern Keenan."

"Trouble!" cried Patrick, astonished. "Now why would a decent reasonable man like meself land in trouble?"

"Ye might meet with a fairy again," Bridget said nervously.

"Well, if I do," said Patrick grandly, "that'll be *one* fairy has met his match."

There was no arguing with Patrick, and when the day of the fair came round he put on his new shoes and his best coat, cocked his hat on his head the way a man does when he thinks well of himself, and whistled up Jess, the hound.

"She'll be company on the road," he said to Bridget, "and

maybe she'll start a hare on the way there or on the way back."

Off he went in great spirits. "I'll bring ye a present from the fair," he shouted back over his shoulder to Bridget, and she waved down the road to him, thinking that she would sooner see him back safe and sound than have the best present the fair could offer.

"You start a hare, me girl," Patrick said to Jess trotting along at his side, "and we'll have hare soup for supper tonight." He smacked his lips at the thought, and Jess, who understood every word he said, danced on her hind legs and barked at him, knowing full well she could run down any hare in Connemara.

All the horse-dealers for miles around were at the fair and Patrick had a fine time of it with them. Everyone listened to his opinions with great respect and no one so much as mentioned the word "flies" though Mulhoy, the cattle-dealer, looked his way once or twice with more than the hint of a smile on his big, round face. Patrick paid no attention to him. "Sure, the man's as ignorant as one of his own cattle beasts," he said to himself.

He was so full of his own importance and so busy talking that he forgot all about Bridget's present until he was on his way home. She'll maybe be content with a hare for the pot, he thought, and sent Jess on ahead, trotting along with her nose to the ground.

It was well after dark now, but the moon was high and the path was clear as Patrick strode along behind Jess, whistling and thinking of his day at the fair and what a fine fellow he was. They went a mile like this and part of another mile, and then Jess flushed a creature out of the grass.

"A hare!" Patrick shouted. "After her, girl!"

Jess needed no telling. She was after the hare like an arrow from a bow, and Patrick after the two of them, racing his shadow across the moonlit grass in great, galumphing strides. "Hare soup!" he bellowed as he pounded on, straining his eyes after hare and dog. Jess was running full out, and the hare in front of her was running like a mad thing and bounding higher than Patrick had ever seen a hare bound before.

"Ah, but she'll catch it, she'll catch it," he shouted exultantly. "She has the legs of any hare in Connemara."

And presently the two creatures in front of him stopped running, and Patrick came panting up to them. And then he found a very strange thing had happened. Jess had not touched the hare. She was lying in front of it, a yard away from the creature, panting gently as she rested her head on her forepaws.

"What's at ye, then?" Patrick shouted crossly.

Then he took a closer look at the hare crouched on its haunches in front of the dog with its long ears laid back from its head, and he whistled in astonishment for the hare was pure white. And even stranger still, around its neck and gleaming in the moonlight against the silky white fur, there was a golden chain. Patrick scratched his head at the sight of his dog lying peacefully in front of the hare, and scratched it harder still at the idea of a white hare with a golden chain round its neck.

"I wonder, now," he said aloud, "is it a pet hare that's got free? And is that why Jess won't touch it, and is that why it wears a golden chain?" He bent down to have a closer look at the hare. "I wonder, now," he said, "is it real gold?" And with a quick movement, he whipped the gold chain over the hare's head.

As he straightened up, the hare moved. In front of his eyes, the shape of it grew blurred till it was like the smoky shadow

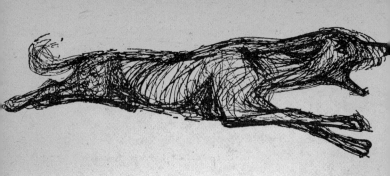

of a hare, and through the smoke, a shape began to form, and the form grew and took on color and substance until it had the likeness of a tall woman.

Her face was pale, her eyes were black, and her hair was black and long and parted in the middle of her brow. Her gown was white, banded with gold, and her black eyes were fixed sternly on Patrick Kentigern Keenan.

All this happened very quickly—so quickly that Patrick's mouth, which had fallen open in astonishment when the shape of the hare began to blur, had not time to close again. All the same, he kept his head and remembered his manners, and snatching off his hat, he made a low bow to the fairy-woman, for that she was a fairy-woman he had no doubt at all.

"I'm sure I ask your pardon, ma'am," he said quickly, "for allowing my hound, Jess, to chase you. But, sure, she's only a dog and I'm only a man, and how on the good earth were we to know that you were a—were a———" and he stopped short, not quite daring to name what he thought she was.

The fairy-woman smiled, and it seemed to Patrick a cold and terrible smile.

"You do well, Patrick, not to name me," she said, and her voice was as musical as water running over stones, but Patrick did not like her voice and he did not like the way she was looking at him either.

"I'll have my necklace back," she said, holding out one slim white hand for it.

Patrick sighed, for he had hoped to be able to keep the necklace, but he handed it over. Just as it touched her fingers she said, "Such a thing should not be in the hands of a stupid, ignorant man like yourself."

"Stupid!" Patrick roared. "Ignorant! There's not a man, woman, or child in Connemara will say that to Patrick Kentigern Keenan. Let me tell you, ma'am, that I happen to be the smartest man in Ireland." He shook his fist at her and fairly danced with rage. "You'd not get *me* roaming over the countryside in the shape of a hare," he bawled furiously, "for I've more sense in my head than you or any fairy in Connemara!"

"Indeed so," said the fairy-woman, smiling a cold little smile. "Are you sure of that, Patrick?"

"Sure, I'm sure," Patrick shouted at her, and suddenly, without another word to warn him, she shot out her arm and dropped the necklace over his head.

As the necklace slid round his neck he heard her cry, "We'll see about that, Patrick." Then he heard no more, for a painful cramp seized the whole of his body. His head swam, his hair seemed to stand on end, and the earth and sky rocked all round him. Then the pain began to ease away and the earth and sky took their proper shape again. Patrick opened his eyes and found to his relief that he was still alive.

The fairy-woman was still in front of him, but she seemed to be much taller than before. And the grass, that had been round his knees, was as high as his face. A yard or two away from him, Jess was rising to her feet and she seemed to Patrick to be as big as a horse. I've shrunk, he thought in dismay. The truth of the matter struck him as Jess leapt forward. The fairy-woman had turned him into a hare. And now his own dog was after him!

Patrick tried to yell, but the sound stuck in his throat. There was nothing for it but to run, and run he did with the fairy-woman's mocking laughter streaming behind him and Jess panting and snuffling on his heels as if it was her dearest wish to catch him. Which, of course, it was.

There was never a stranger sight in Ireland than that night when Patrick Kentigern Keenan was chased over the moonlit grass by his own dog, and never a man with greater terror in his heart than Patrick. He leaped and twisted and turned. He jumped over bushes and slithered through hedges. He scudded along at a pace that nearly broke his heart, and still Jess was behind him. Over and over again he heard her teeth snap together just short of his flying heels, and the sheer fright of it drove him to run at a speed that was nothing less than a miracle.

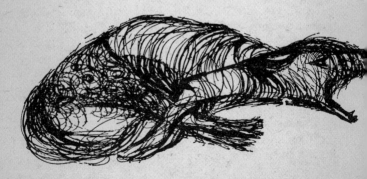

He dared not stop. He had no breath left to cry out to the dog and even if he had—would it be a man's voice that would come out of his mouth or only a hare's squeal? There was nothing for it but to try and make the safety of his own front door. It was not far now. He could see the dark outline of the house in the moonlight, and glory be, Bridget was up and about. There was a light streaming out of the front door.

With a last despairing bound, Patrick got halfway up the garden path, and with a last mighty leap, Jess was on top of him. Her warm weight crushed him down. Her teeth clicked in the fur of his throat. His mouth opened wide in a yell of terror, he jerked his neck violently away from the dog's teeth, and the fairy necklace shot over his head and fell to the ground.

Patrick never heard what sort of sound came from his throat and he would not know to this day whether it was a hare's squeal or a man's shout, for the instant that the fairy necklace fell off his neck and rolled to the ground, the pain that had seized him before fell on him again. His head swam, his hair stood on end, and the earth and sky rocked all round him. In the middle of it all, he heard Bridget's astonished voice.

"Patrick," she was shouting, "what in the wide world are

you up to, rollin' around on the ground with Jess on top of you?"

"Save me, Bridget, save me," Patrick screamed at the top of his voice, and keeping his eyes screwed shut against the sight of the hound's jaws at his throat.

"Save you from what?" cried Bridget.

"I'm a hare, woman. Can't you see I'm a hare?" roared Patrick, and to his horror, Bridget began to laugh.

"A hare, is it?" she cried. "Then you'll do fine for the pot."

Patrick howled with terror at that. His eyes flew open and there was Bridget standing over him, laughing, with a candle in her hand. Jess was still lying on his chest and Patrick gave another yell at the sight of her. He thrust out his hands to push her away, and the truth struck him again. He was back in his own shape. He pushed Jess off his chest and staggered to his feet, groaning and sighing and feeling tenderly at all his aching muscles and stretched joints.

"Ah, ye treacherous brute," he said angrily to Jess as she tried to lick his face, and just then Bridget saw the gold necklace lying on the ground.

"Oh, Patrick, ye dear man," she cried. "Now I forgive ye all your foolish faults for the fine present you've brought me."

She darted forward and picked up the necklace.

"Wait, Bridget! Wait!" Patrick cried, but he was too late. Bridget had already hung the necklace round her neck. She ran into the house, laughing and chattering and went straight up to the mirror. "Bridget, Bridget! Oh, what will happen to me poor wife?" Patrick moaned. He hobbled after her, horror-struck and expecting to see hare's ears sprouting from her head any minute. But a different thing altogether happened to Bridget.

As Patrick looked over her shoulder at her reflection in the mirror, her whole face seemed to light up with the gleam and

sparkle of the gold chain at her throat. Her dark hair shone with the sudden gleam of a blackbird's wing glancing in the sun. A rising color flushed her cheeks to the velvety pink of an opening rose, and like a dusky rose smiling in the candlelight she turned to him, and from the happiness of her strange new beauty she cried:

"Oh, Patrick! Am I not the luckiest woman in Ireland?"

Not a word could Patrick Kentigern Keenan say, for his breath was quite taken away at the sight of her. "You are that!" was all he could manage when the breath came back into his throat again, and he sat down, not able to take his eyes off her. Jess came and laid her head on his knee as he sat staring, and he put the tip of his finger against her sharp teeth and shuddered as he remembered how they had clicked and snapped only an inch or two from his heels.

"And yet ye couldn't catch me, girl," he said, and smiled with satisfaction. The smile became a laugh, for Patrick had suddenly remembered himself rolling on the ground screaming, "I'm a hare! I'm a hare!" when all the time he was back in his own shape again.

Bridget turned round from the mirror, smiling and thinking he was laughing for pleasure at the sight of her wearing the necklace, but Patrick was pointing at Jess and laughing so much by this time that she was afraid he would choke.

"For the dear sake, Patrick," she cried, alarmed, "have you lost your wits?" And she ran to fetch him a drink of water.

"No," said Patrick, sobering down a bit, "but I nearly lost me life. Put your finger against that dog's teeth, Bridget."

"I don't know what to make of this at all," said Bridget, but she felt Jess's teeth all the same. "They're sharp as needles," she said, drawing her finger away in a hurry.

"That's why I'm laughin', Bridget," Patrick said, grinning

down at her. "Maybe you are the luckiest woman in Ireland
tonight, me dear, but when ye consider the sharpness of that
hound's teeth, there isn't a doubt about it, I'm the luckiest
man."

4

The Silver Bridle

You can't beat a woman's curiosity, and in no time at all Bridget had the story of the gold necklace out of Patrick. When she had heard the whole thing from beginning to end, she took the necklace off, and one look in the mirror was enough to tell her that the beauty it had given her was gone.

"Are ye not goin' to wear it, then?" Patrick demanded. "And me after bein' nearly killed to get it for you!"

"I'll wear it sometimes," Bridget said. She slipped it round her neck again and smiled to see the strange and lovely face that looked back at her out of the glass. "But only sometimes." With a little sigh, she took the necklace off for the last time and put it carefully away. "That way," she said, "it will be a greater surprise for me to be so beautiful, and a greater pleasure for you to look at me."

Patrick grumbled on for a while, but in the end, "Ah well, maybe you're right at that," he said, for the truth was, he was beginning to see that Bridget had a great deal of sense to her.

"And, Patrick," said Bridget, "take a lesson from the white hare. You nearly came to grief over it, and grief's all you'll get if you go on trying to prove yourself smarter than the fairies."

"Haven't I three times met with a fairy and no harm done?" Patrick demanded. "There's my new shoes, and the golden spoon, and now the golden necklace to prove it."

"And the fairy got the better of you every time," Bridget reminded him.

"I made a vow," Patrick said stubbornly, "and I'll keep that vow. I'll prove yet that I'm the smartest man in Ireland."

But though he talked so big and so bold, the white hare had given Patrick a bigger fright than he cared to admit, and what with that and the greater respect he had for Bridget's good sense, he was content for a while to stay at home and mind his own business. It couldn't last, of course, and in spite of all Bridget's warnings, Patrick took up with his old ways of wandering abroad again and poking his long nose into things that would have been better left alone.

And so it happened one night that he was walking late by himself when he saw a light ahead of him. It was not standing still as you might have expected, but moving slowly away. As soon as he saw it, nothing would do Patrick but he must find out where it was and what it was.

He began to walk toward it, and as he moved, the light moved so that he never seemed to get any nearer to it, but Patrick was a stubborn man and this only made him all the more determined to find out what it was. He began to run, not looking where he was going, and suddenly his feet squelched in water and he was up to his knees in a bog.

Muttering angrily to himself, he pulled one foot clear and stepped forward, but the next step was bog, too, and the next, and the next again, until it dawned on him that he was in the middle of a bog and had not the least idea where to go to get out of it. Fright fairly took him by the hair then, for he realized that the light had only been a bog-light—the flame that is sometimes seen on marshes and that people say is lit by the fairies to lure men to their death in the bog.

"Ah, but they'll not get me so easy," muttered Patrick when he had got over the first shock. "Not me that's the smartest man in Ireland."

He felt around himself in the mud till he found a long, tough root. Then he pulled himself up onto a tussock of grass and thrust the root down into the soft, oozy ground around him, testing for the firmest spot. In this way, he moved forward, always testing the next step with his foot before he ventured to leave the hold he had, and after a while he was on firm ground again, very cold and wet and tired but still free of the bog and very full of his own cleverness at the way he had done it.

At the same time, there was no denying that he was lost, and with the bog between him and the way he had come, he would have to wait for the morning light before he could find his way home. But walk he must or he would freeze in his wet clothes, and so he struck off, always keeping to the rising ground for fear of falling into a bog again. It was when he had been walking like this for an hour, stamping his feet now and then to keep warm, that he suddenly remembered what day—or rather, what night—it was. Midsummer's Eve. And he had chosen that night, the night of all the year when fairies were most likely to be abroad, to wander far from home and get lost into the bargain.

"Well," he said to himself, "there's nothing for it but to keep a sharp lookout and be ready for trouble if it comes." And so he walked on with his ears pricked and his eyes darting hither and thither to see what they could see. The moon came up and shone white on the grass around him, and Patrick stopped to look about.

Suddenly he heard a noise like music, very faint and far away, and with it, another sound like thunder very far off. The sound got louder and nearer, and straining his ears to listen, Patrick realized what it was. The music was the sound of hundreds of little bells tinkling, and the thunder was the sound of horses' hoofs on the turf.

Common sense told Patrick to get down out of sight of whatever or whoever was coming his way, but curiosity kept him on his feet till the very last second before the horses he had heard came in sight. As they breasted the skyline, he ducked quickly into a fold in the ground and lay there, holding his breath and wishing he were back home again beside the fire with Bridget telling him all his faults, for he knew then that he was about to see what few people had ever seen, and that was a company of fairy horsemen riding abroad on Midsummer's Eve.

They swept by, only a few feet away from him, and him pressed into the ground as if he was growing there like the grass, but still with curiosity fighting his fear enough to let him raise his head now and then to see what they were like. What he saw made his eyes stand out like a frog's.

Every single horse that flew past was as white as new snow; their hoofs were like polished black steel and they were shod with silver, and from the bridle-rein of every horse and from the trappings of each saddle hung dozens of little silver bells that swung and tinkled with a wild, sweet music in time with their flying hoofs.

Not a sight of a face did Patrick see of the men and women that mounted the white horses, but now and then he saw the sweep of a green robe, the toe of a shining shoe, and a stream of gold as a fairy-woman's hair flew out behind her. He dared not raise his eyes further to see more, and when they had passed he kept still for a while, not knowing if more of the fairy troop might be coming that way. No more horses

came, but it seemed to Patrick that he could hear voices. He rose cautiously to his knees and looked over the rim of the hollow. The fairy troop had stopped not a hundred yards from him, the riders had dismounted, and their horses were grazing quietly a little way off from where they had gathered together. As Patrick watched, the fairy-people formed themselves into a circle and began to dance and sing, with one of their number standing in the middle of the circle and playing on a silver pipe.

"Did you ever," said Patrick to himself, "see the beat of that!" He lay with his chin on his hands watching the dancers twirling and jumping. There was not a soul would believe him if he swore with his hand on his heart that he had seen such a thing happen, he thought. The dance grew faster. The dancers were spinning like tops, the circle breaking and forming again with each new movement of the dance.

It was when he noticed that the dancers were moving farther and farther away from the horses that a wild idea came into Patrick's head. If he could capture one of these great white horses for his own, there was not a man, woman, or child in Ireland but would believe the tale of what he had seen.

Patrick Kentigern Keenan was a man of action. No sooner had the thought come into his head than he began to move

forward on his hands and knees. Luck was with him, for as he crawled toward the herd, one of the horses began to wander off on its own. Patrick changed his direction so that he would be between this horse and the herd when it tried to return, and inched along behind it, hardly able to breathe with excitement.

"Just let me capture you, my beauty," he muttered, "and there's no one will deny that I'm the smartest man in Ireland."

Now he was close up to it. He turned cautiously to look at the fairy company. They were still dancing in a ring, laughing and singing, with their horses cropping quietly. He was alone with the white horse.

He lay in the grass and looked long and lovingly at it; at the coat that gleamed like white satin, at the great muscles moving smoothly under the shining skin, at the mane as soft

and white as dandelion floss flowing over the proud, arched
neck. Light and delicate as a dancer on its long, slim legs, it
stepped over the grass and the little silver bells on its bridle-
rein rang with faint music.

Patrick's stomach drew into a tight knot of excitement. He
rose to his knees, and the white horse turned its head in his
direction. Its pointed ears flicked forward.

It was now or never. Slowly and carefully he drew his
feet up under him, crouched for a second as tense as a coiled
spring, then leapt forward. One bound took him to the
horse's side. With one hand he clutched its mane, and laid
hold of the pommel of the saddle with the other. It reared
on its hind legs, nostrils flaring, lips drawn back over its teeth
in a snicker of alarm, and as its forefeet struck the ground
again Patrick was up in the saddle, his knees pressed close
into the horse's flanks, the reins gathered in his left hand.

"Hup! Away!" he roared, and brought his right hand hard
down on its hindquarters. Then he clutched the reins with
both hands and hung on for dear life as the fairy horse
bounded forward as if it had been shot from a gun.

Shouts sounded behind him, and the sound of horses' hoofs.
A hail of arrows came over his head, whining past him like
bees—tiny arrows with deadly, poison-tipped barbs, and Patrick, groaning with fear when he wasn't shouting with excitement, bent low over the white horse's neck and said to
himself, "Oh, if I'm not the biggest fool in Ireland!"

But Patrick Kentigern Keenan knew horseflesh, you had to
say that for him, and he had stolen the strongest and the
fleetest of the fairy horses. The shouts grew fainter, the arrows
began to fall short, and soon he was alone, thundering along
in the moonlight, mounted as no man had ever been mounted
before or since.

Low over ditches the white horse skimmed. High it
soared over hedges and plunged downwards like a thunder-

bolt to the earth again. The wind got up and whipped ragged
clouds forward across the sky, but fast as the ragged clouds
raced, the white horse outpaced them.

Uphill or downhill was all the same to it. The air whistled
past Patrick's ears as it bounded forward with gigantic strides.
His hat flew off, his teeth jarred with every bounce in the saddle. He tried with all his strength to pull the beast to a halt,
but with a toss of its head and a powerful pull on the reins,
the fairy-horse nearly jerked his arms from their sockets,
and it began to dawn on Patrick that the white horse would
never tire of the speed it was going and that no human rider
could ever pull it to a halt.

A cold sweat broke out on his forehead. Could he throw
himself off its back? No. At that pace he would break his
neck. But what was to happen to him? Was he doomed to
gallop forever the length and breadth of Ireland, astride this
wild, white creature? Was that to be his punishment for
stealing a fairy-horse?

On and on in the white moonlight the white horse sped.
Valleys and hills dropped behind them. A wide, winding
river barred their path and hope shot through Patrick. But
the white horse gathered itself and leapt from bank to bank
as if the wide river had been a little stream. Patrick lost all
count of time. His hands were numb on the reins, his head
was spinning like a top. If ever I get home safe and sound, he
vowed, I'll never lay hands again on a thing that's not right-
fully mine. And he groaned to think that he was maybe hundreds of miles from home.

A village rose out of the darkness in front of them. The
white horse took the row of houses in a bound and thundered on. The thought of people peacefully asleep in their
beds and him soaring over them clinging like a burr to the
back of the fairy-horse sent Patrick nearly wild with temper.

"Help! Help!" he roared, twisting his neck to look back

at the houses. Not a sound came from the village, not a house
showed a glimmer of light. "I'm done for!" Patrick groaned,
and just at that moment a cock crowed shrilly in the distance.

The white horse stopped dead in its tracks at the sound
and, taken by surprise, Patrick shot out of the saddle and
clean over its head. He had just time to think, as he spun
through the air, that this was a sad end for a great man like
himself to come to when he struck the ground and knew no

more. And as he lay there on the ground, the cock crowed again and the fairy-horse vanished like a puff of smoke blown down the wind.

Now it would take more than a fall from a horse to kill a man like Patrick Kentigern Keenan. He opened his eyes again at last to find that the white horse had vanished and that he was lying on the soft earth of a potato patch. It was growing to full daylight now, with cocks answering the one that had crowed, from all over the place. Patrick raised himself on his elbow and looked around, and to his great astonishment saw that it was his own potato patch he had landed in.

"Well, that's great good fortune I dug this ground yesterday," he said, "or a fall like that would have been the end of me right enough."

Then he saw that he was holding something in his hand, and that something was the silver bridle of the fairy-horse.

"Well, if that doesn't beat all!" he said. "I must have held on so tight that the beast had to slip its bridle before it could vanish on me."

He lay there for a while to get over his aches and pains, feeling the shine and weight of the silver bridle in his hands and admiring his own courage in holding onto it in spite of the fairy-horse. Then he got up and limped into the house for his breakfast.

Bridget had plenty to say to him when he came in all covered with earth and his clothes all torn and his hat missing, but Patrick ate his breakfast with the silver bridle on the table in front of him, and he was so busy thinking of the cunning and the courage it had taken to win it that he never heard a word she said.

It was not long after this that a farmer came to him with a wild young horse and asked him to break it. "For I'll have to shoot it if you can't, Patrick," he said. "It's no use in the world to me the way it is, for there isn't a man that can handle it."

"You've come to the one man that can," said Patrick, though he didn't like the wild, rolling eye of the horse nor the way it jerked its head against the halter. "Get its head well down, man."

The farmer pulled tight on the halter-rope, the horse's head came down, and Patrick threw the silver bridle over it. Well, as soon as the creature felt the touch of the fairy bridle, it stopped its rearing and prancing and stood as still as a stone for Patrick to mount it. He walked that horse, he cantered, he galloped, and you would have thought it had been ridden for years the way it answered to his lightest touch.

"Well, if that doesn't beat all!" gasped the farmer. He was so surprised that he paid Patrick more than he had meant to, and when he got home he spread the word that there wasn't a man in Ireland could tame horses like Patrick Kentigern Keenan.

Patrick's fame as a horse-breaker spread all over the land and horses were brought from far and near for him to tame. But it wasn't long before people began to notice that the silver bridle had more to do with it than he had. He was questioned upside down and inside out to know how he had come by it, but he said never a word except, "I'm the smartest man in Ireland, and that means that I know when to hold my tongue."

He was sorely tempted to tell the story of the fairy-horse, but he had sense enough to see that no one would believe it after the business of Mulhoy and the fairy cattle. "Let them wonder," he said to himself. "Sure, wonder's good for the soul and there'll come a day when I can speak out loud and clear to show the whole of Connemara the cleverness that's in me."

Bridget was the only one that ever got the true story of

the silver bridle out of him, and though she didn't know what Patrick was thinking to himself, she was pleased at the way he answered all the curious questions about it. "You're learnin' sense, Patrick," she said, smiling. "I do believe you're learnin' sense at last."

And still Patrick said never a word. Which shows that he had learned a deal more sense than even Bridget gave him credit for.

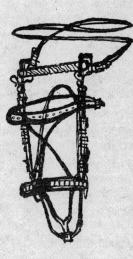

5
The
Blue
Stone

FIRST PART

Some folks learn easy, and the ones like Patrick Kentigern Keenan that have a high opinion of themselves learn the hard way. The new shoes had given his pride a tumble; the golden spoon had shown him that kindness wins over cleverness; the golden necklace had warned him of the danger of speaking out of turn; and the silver bridle had taught him to bide his time. But he was still a terrible boaster for all that.

When Bridget brought out the golden spoon on holidays and put it beside Kieron's place at the table, Patrick would smile down at the little boy and say, "And who is fitter to sup with a golden spoon than the son of Patrick Kentigern Keenan!"

A terrible boaster and a proud man, that was Patrick. Still, you couldn't blame him for being proud of Kieron who was growing up to be a fine little boy, with dark eyes that showed the amount of mischief in him and the same natural ability for getting into trouble as his father.

He was the darling of Patrick's heart, and because of the

great love he had for the boy, he grew gentler and kinder in all his ways as Kieron grew older, for small ones like him take a deal of patience in the handling. Indeed, Bridget wondered sometimes at the patience a man of his quick temper showed. She was all for sending Kieron to the Abbey so that the Fathers could teach him his letters.

"That'll clip his wings," she said, but Patrick wouldn't hear of being parted from him.

"You spoil the boy," said Bridget, but she wasn't far behind, herself, when it came to spoiling, and she was as proud as Patrick himself to see the big, shining spoon grasped in Kieron's small hand.

There came a day, though, when Bridget wished she had never seen the golden spoon, for it became a great danger and temptation to Patrick. Gold and gleaming as it was, it put him in mind of other gold in other places, and every time he looked at it, winking and glittering against the scrubbed white of the table, he would fall to dreaming of the secret store of gold that the fairies were said to keep buried under the hearthstones of their houses in the hills.

From dreaming of it, he fell to talking of it and of the fairy-houses that he had heard tell of from his grandfather, Sylvanus Keenan, a man that knew more about the fairies of Ireland than any man living.

"Half under the ground they are," he said, "and round like a beehive, with turf growin' over the roof so you'd never think it was a fairy-house you were seein' but only a low mound in the hills. And that's where they keep their gold, boy, under the hearthstones of the low green houses in the middle-earth of the hills."

"Ah, but it's not real gold," said Bridget, "for it will turn to dead leaves in your hand the next sunrise after you've got it."

"Indeed so!" said Patrick, lifting the golden spoon. "This

spoon has seen a few sunrises then, and there's not much of the dead leaf about it." He waved the spoon under Bridget's nose. "And the gold of your necklace—that's good, hard, solid gold, isn't it? No, no," said he, "never tell me fairy gold isn't true gold—not when I've seen it and touched it with my own hands."

"But they can *turn* it to dead leaves," said Bridget.

"Aha!" said Patrick cunningly, "but not if they don't know who has it."

And feeling very pleased with himself that he had won the argument, he took up his stick, clapped his hat on his head, and strolled out into the sunshine to think things over.

It was a fine morning, with the dew still thick on the long grass and the sun making blue shadows in the folds of the hills. Patrick strode along with his stick over his shoulder and his hat on the side of his head, taking long steps so that he could admire his feet in the leprechaun's shoes. The farther he walked, the more the idea grew in his head that if he could only find again the fairy-houses that his grandfather had seen in the hills, he would think of some way to get the fairies' gold without their being a bit the wiser who had run off with it.

"I have the day before me," he said aloud, "and who is to know what may happen before the day is out?"

He stopped and looked at the low, misty line of the hills. In his mind's eye, he could see the beehive houses with their turf roofs, and far below them in the dark earth, the glitter of gold.

"I'll do it," he vowed.

He settled his hat on his head, squared his shoulders, pursed his lips for a whistle, and strode off smartly in the direction of the hills. There was no thought in his mind of Bridget, not even of little Kieron. He did not see the larks that sprang up from the soft grass under his feet nor hear their song showering down from the sky. All his mind was bent to one purpose, and that was to win the fairies' gold.

Stories crowded into his mind as he walked—stories he had heard as a little boy from his grandfather. "They are a small people, the fairies," old Sylvanus used to say, "but not so small, Patrick, that they cannot sometimes be mistaken for mortal folk, and their queen is a woman so fair that no man who has once seen her face can forget it. They can change at will to any shape they please. They can be plain in your sight one minute and in the next can vanish like a puff of smoke or a straw blown down the wind. They have power over cattle and humankind, and can make a cow run dry or a baby vanish from its cradle. And who they capture, they spirit away to be their bond-slaves forever in their houses in the middle-earth of the hills."

Just for a moment as he thought of this, Patrick's heart stood still and it was as if a cold wind had blown over him. But the next minute his courage rose again. He thumped his stick on the ground.

"I'm the bravest man in Ireland," said Patrick Kentigern Keenan. And indeed that might have been true, for it took a brave man to do what he was doing that day.

The day was hot and getting hotter. The ground was steep and getting steeper, and Patrick was glad when he came to a stream and could sit down and dabble his hands in the cool water. He splashed some on his face, and was just about to cup his hands to take a drink when he heard children's voices shouting and the sound of splashing. He looked toward the sound and saw that farther down the stream there was a line of stepping-stones. An old woman was crossing on them, and though her steps were shaky, a group of boys who stood on the bank were throwing stones into the stream and laughing as she shrank back from the spurts of water and almost lost her footing.

Now, foolish and lazy and boastful as he was, there was one thing that Patrick Kentigern Keenan could not abide and that was cruelty in any shape or form. With a roar of rage he jumped to his feet, seized his stick, and ran to the boys, whirling it round his head.

"Shame! Shame on ye to torment a poor old woman that could be your grandmother!" he roared. "Oh, wait till I get a cut at your legs, me boyos! We'll see who jumps then!"

"Run! Run!" the boys shouted, and were off like hares through the long grass, yelling as Patrick's stick came thumping about them.

"Ah, ye have the legs of me," said Patrick, knowing well that he could never catch such swift creatures but well content to have given them such a fright, and he turned back to the stream and hurried to help the old woman over to the other bank.

"Are ye all right now, ma'am?" he asked gallantly as he set her down on the other side.

"I am indeed, sir, and thank you kindly for your help," said the old woman, but she kept her head down so that her bonnet hid her face and spoke so low that Patrick could hardly hear her.

Poor old soul, he thought, she's frightened half to death. And when the old woman asked him timidly if he would walk a piece of the way with her, he agreed without a thought.

"And which is your way, ma'am?" he asked.

The old woman heaved the bundle she had with her onto her back and pointed to the path that Patrick himself was taking.

"Ah, our roads are the same," said Patrick, quite well pleased that doing this kindness for the old woman was not going to lose him any time, and he stepped out briskly again.

But the old woman was a slow walker and she took two steps for every one of his, so that if he walked at his ordinary pace, she had to trot along beside him, and if he walked at hers, it seemed to him that he was only dawdling along.

"Have ye far to go, ma'am?" he asked, not feeling nearly so kindly to her now.

"Not far," said the old woman, and she had such a weak, thin voice that Patrick felt ashamed of his impatience and suited his pace to hers.

The old woman walked slower and slower. She shifted her bundle from her back and carried it on one arm and then on the other and sighed and muttered to herself.

"Here, let me carry your bundle, ma'am," said Patrick. He took it off her arm and swung it onto his back. There was hardly any weight in it at all.

"Ah, it's fine to be strong," the old woman said wearily.

"That's true," Patrick agreed, "and I'm not saying so, mind you, but it may be, it may well be that I'm the strongest man in Ireland."

They walked on at the old woman's pace with Patrick carrying the bundle and her trudging beside him with her hands inside her sleeves and her head bent down so that her bonnet hid her face. Never a word did she say to all of Patrick's talk, but sometimes she sighed and shook her head and when he asked how far she had to go, she always said, "Not far," and pointed on the way he would have gone himself.

And so, at last, Patrick gave up trying to make cheerful conversation. He whistled a tune to himself as he walked along in step to the old woman's slow step. All the while he was trying not to think about the ache that was growing in his back, for the bundle he was carrying was not as light as a feather now. It was heavy and getting heavier at every step, or so it seemed to Patrick, and soon the sweat was running down his face and it was all he could do to stop from groaning aloud with the weight of it pressing into his back. Suddenly, the old woman said:

"You've carried my bundle a good piece, sir. Let me take it now."

Patrick was sorely tempted. But how could he let an old woman carry a load that was nearly killing him?

"No, no," he said between his teeth, " 'tis too heavy by far for you, ma'am," and he shuffled along bent nearly double with the weight of it.

At last he could bear it no longer. He stopped, and swung the bundle to the ground. "You must be needing a rest, ma'am," he said, ashamed to say that it was the weight of the bundle that had stopped him. "We'll stop here for a minute."

The old woman sat down on the grass with never a thank you, and Patrick felt his temper rising. The old creature was

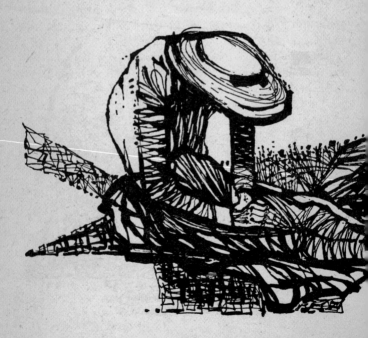

leading him a fine dance with her "Not far now," and hour after hour slipping away while they plodded along as slow as two old donkeys! He looked longingly around him at the hills rising in every direction. Somewhere, somewhere in these hills were the smooth green mounds of the fairy-houses, somewhere was the glitter of the fairy gold.

He drew in his breath to speak as he looked down at the old woman. She was looking up at him and for the first time he saw her face. It was small and brown and so wrinkled

that it looked like a rock that had seen a thousand summers and weathered a thousand winters, and her eyes were brown and sad, like the eyes of an old dog when it knows its master is going to leave it.

"I have only a little way to go now, sir," said the old woman. "You'll not leave me now, will you, all by myself in this wild lonely place?"

Patrick looked at the sun that had begun to swing round to the west. If he stayed with her there would not be time to make the search he had in mind before darkness overtook him, and who would be alone in these hills when the dark came and the fairies' magic was at its strongest! He must leave her now, before it was too late. He took a deep breath and looked down to tell her that he must go on alone. The brown, wrinkled face, with a line in it for every sorrow in the tired old eyes, looked up at him, and all his stern impatience melted away in the sudden warmth of pity he felt for the sadness that was in it.

"Sure, I wouldn't desert a lady, ma'am," said Patrick Kentigern Keenan, and he swung the bundle onto his back again.

The old woman rose to her feet and they trudged on in silence for another hour. The bundle didn't seem so heavy now and Patrick thought that maybe he had got used to the weight. But still, he was glad when the old woman stopped beside a stretch of stunted thorn trees.

"This is the end of the road," she said.

Patrick swung the bundle off his back and looked around him. There were no houses to be seen, no people, no fields. He looked to north, south, and east, and there was only bare hillside. He looked west into the light of the setting sun, and there was only the thorn trees, bent and twisted into strange shapes round a green, grassy mound.

"Where would ye be goin', then, ma'am?" he asked. "There's neither house nor hall to be seen."

"I am going to my home," the old woman said.

It was on the tip of Patrick's tongue then to ask her where her home was, but suddenly he noticed that the branches of the thorn trees were like bare, twisted arms with thorns like sharp fingers clawing the air. No birds sang in that place, not a rustle from a blade of grass broke the strange stillness of the air and Patrick was suddenly afraid.

The old woman held out her hand for the bundle and Patrick gave it to her, glad to think he was going to see the back of her at last.

"I'll say good day, ma'am," he said, raising his hat.

"Wait," she said. "You have been kind—so kind. I am thinking what I might give you."

"For the dear sake!" said Patrick, surprised. "And what would I be takin' for helpin' a poor old body carry her bundle on a lonely piece of road!"

"I will give you this," said the old woman.

She held out her hand. On her rough, brown palm there lay a piece of stone about the size and shape of a small egg, round and smooth as if from much handling and of a curious dull blue color. Patrick looked from the stone to the old woman and was about to smile, for he was sure now that she was soft in the head to offer him a piece of stone, but being a kindly man he did not like to hurt her feelings.

"Now, my little boy, Kieron, would like to have a stone like that to play with," he said, and he took it from her.

"Yes," said the old woman, "give it to the one that needs it most."

She swung her bundle onto her back and trudged off toward the thorn bushes.

6
The
Blue
Stone

SECOND PART

Patrick Kentigern Keenan watched the old woman go, wondering which road she would take. She walked straight in among the thorn bushes, though there was no path that he could see through them, and he waited for her to come out on the other side. The sun dazzled his eyes, but even so, there was no sign of the old woman again.

"That's queer," he said. "Where on the earth did she get to?"

Still, he had no time to stand and stare. He was very hungry and he would have to hurry to get home before dark. He was tired, too, and out of temper as he walked home, for it had been a wasted day after all. Yet it would have gone against the grain not to have helped the old woman, queer and all as she was, even though she had stopped him doing what he had set out to do.

Hunger began to twist his stomach into a knot, and he lengthened his stride, thinking that he would give all the fairies' gold at that moment for a good big meal. And so, empty-handed except for the blue stone that lay forgotten in his pocket, Patrick reached home well after dark.

Bridget met him at the door and one look at her face was enough to tell him there was trouble in the house.

"It's Kieron," she whispered. "He's sick, Patrick. He ate poison berries. I've sent to the Abbey for Brother Simon, the apothecary."

Patrick's heart gave a great thud. He ran inside and stopped by Kieron's bed, and Bridget followed him, moaning and wiping her tearful face. Kieron lay tossing and turning on the bed, the blankets all twisted round him. His face was fiery and burning hot to the touch. His eyes were wide and staring. Patrick bent over him.

"Kieron, it's your Da," he said softly. "Speak to me, Kieron." But the little boy only whimpered and twisted away from him.

Patrick swallowed down a great lump in his throat. "What kind of berries was it?" he asked Bridget.

She took a branch off the table and handed it to him. The clusters of purple berries on it looked almost black in the dim light of the lamp, and Patrick's heart sank when he saw them. The Abbey was far away and Brother Simon would come too late to help his little Kieron, for it was a deadly poison that filled the smooth, shining skins of these berries.

"Have you purged him and bled him?" he asked Bridget.

"Yes, I have. What can we do, Patrick, what can we do?" cried poor Bridget.

Patrick had not the heart to tell her that there was nothing more to be done. He bent down and wrapped the blankets round the little boy. Then he lifted him out of bed and sat down by the fire with the child in his arms.

"We must wait for Brother Simon," he said quietly.

Bridget sat down beside him, and they both stared into the fire and waited, saying nothing. Patrick's mind drifted this way and that. He thought of Kieron, and of himself as a little boy in that very house in front of the same fire. He thought of himself sitting on his grandfather's knee as Kieron now sat on his, and the old man talking, talking away, telling stories by the hour. Strange stories that only an old man would know and only a little boy would remember.

Soon, with the heat of the child in his arms and the strain of waiting, the sweat started out on Patrick's brow. He reached into his pocket for his handkerchief and drew out the blue stone along with it. I was going to give it to Kieron for a

toy, he thought. He turned the stone over and over in his fingers, wondering at the curious shape and color of it, and suddenly, as clearly as if the old man had been in the room, he remembered a story that his grandfather had once told him.

"There was a thing that used to happen long ago," the old man had said, "in the days before Saint Patrick drove the snakes out of Ireland. And it was only once every seven years that this thing happened. When the sun struck warm on the earth for the first time in the year and the new grass was only a soft, thin carpet on the hard ground, all the serpents in the country left the holes in the rocks and the deep lairs in the ground where they had slept the winter away. They went softly and silently on a journey, not stopping on the way and never striking at anyone that might cross their path, and at the end of the journey, all the snakes in the country were gathered in the one place.

"When they met in this place, they formed a pattern with their bodies and moved as if they were making the movements of a dance. And in the dance, the heads of the serpents all met and touched and they hissed, all at the one time, and the sound was so loud that it seemed the earth itself had given a great sigh. And at this moment of meeting a drop of fluid came from the mouth of each serpent, and all these drops ran together and fell to the ground in the shape of an egg, an egg that turned smooth and hard as stone and took on a dull blue color that no other stone in the world has. Then the serpents went back their several ways and only the stone was left there, lying on the soft thin carpet of the green grass."

Patrick opened his hand and looked at the stone lying there, smooth and round and hard, and a dull blue color that was like no other color he had ever seen before. He thought of the old woman who had hidden her face from him and tried his patience so sorely with her heavy bundle before she had given him the blue stone. He thought of the way she had disappeared so strangely into the empty silence of the hillside and he began to shake all over for he remembered his grandfather's voice saying, "No man has ever found this stone, Patrick, but they do say that a fairy-woman may give it in a gift to a mortal who has shown great kindness of heart, for the stone is called the Stone of Healing and it has the power to cure all illness."

Patrick looked down at Kieron's fevered face. "Give it to the one that needs it most," the old woman had said. Very gently, Patrick placed the blue stone against Kieron's hand and closed the child's fingers round it. He closed his eyes and breathed softly, hardly daring to think what might happen.

The next thing he knew was Bridget's voice in his ear calling, "Patrick! Patrick!"

Patrick gave a great start and opened his eyes. The next instant he was on his feet with a bellow of alarm.

"Kieron! Where is Kieron?" he shouted. "What's happened, woman?"

Bridget laughed. "Look there," she said, pointing to the bed.

Patrick looked. Then he rubbed his eyes and looked again. It was broad daylight, and Kieron was lying in his bed, peacefully asleep. Patrick touched his face and it was cool again, all the fever gone.

"What happened?" he asked, bewildered.

"You fell asleep with the boy in your arms," Bridget told him, "and when I found the fever had left him, I hadn't the heart to wake you, so I just put him back in his bed and let you sleep on."

Patrick bent down to look at Kieron. The child lay with one hand under his rosy cheek; the other lay outside the covers and clutched in the fingers was the blue stone.

"He has had that stone in his hand all night," said Bridget. "Ever since you put it into his fingers."

Patrick went over to the door and stood looking out. He watched the sun roll up the morning mists over the hills and paint blue shadows in their folds. All the things that had happened on his long walk the day before came back into his mind, and as he stood there remembering the old woman and thinking of Kieron so quietly asleep after the night's fever, he knew for certain that he had met with a fairy-woman and that the stone clutched in Kieron's hand was the Stone of Healing.

Bridget came up to him as he stood there, and softly she asked, "Patrick, are you not glad Kieron is well again?"

"I am, Bridget, indeed I am. I'm the happiest man in the whole of Ireland this minute," Patrick cried, and he gave her a great hug.

"Well, then, what is it that troubles ye?" Bridget asked gently, for she could see plainly that he had something on his mind, and Patrick was only too glad to tell her the story of the blue stone and how he had come by it.

"Now here's the puzzle, Bridget," he said when he had got to the end of the tale. "Me granda always said that the stone might be given in a gift from the fairies to one that had shown great kindness of heart, but sure, I did nothin' out of the way for the old woman. It would have been shame on me with the health and strength I have not to have carried her bundle and walked a piece of the way with her."

"Do you not think it was a strange thing," said Bridget, "that you should meet with a fairy-woman, and you on your way to steal the fairies' gold?"

"Maybe so," said Patrick uneasily.

Bridget went on, "And, Patrick, was it not strange, too, that her bundle grew so heavy? And was it not the strangest thing of all that it was meeting with her, walking with her, and carrying her bundle stopped you doing what you set out to do?"

Patrick looked at her in sudden fear. "Bridget," he said, "are ye tellin' me that the fairy-woman knew what I had in mind? Did she come to me on purpose in the shape of a sorrowful old woman, and walk slow and feeble on purpose to stop me getting to the fairy-houses before dark?"

"I am sure of it," said Bridget. "She knew where you were going, Patrick, and she knew the greed for gold that was in your heart."

"But I could have left her," Patrick cried. "I could have run on by myself and reached the fairy-houses while it was still broad day."

"But you stayed with her," said Bridget. "You lost your chance of the gold rather than let an old woman walk weary on a long and lonely road. I think that's why she gave you the blue stone, Patrick."

Patrick walked over to Kieron's bed and stood looking down at the sleeping boy. "I've been rewarded better than I deserve," he said soberly.

"No, Patrick, it was a just reward." Bridget came up to him and put her hand over his. "It's a great kindness indeed," she said, "that is greater than the greed for gold, and it took a fairy-woman to see the truth of *that*."

"To think I walked beside her," said Patrick, "all unknowing she was a fairy-woman, and took from her as if it had been a worthless pebble a gift more precious than all the fairy gold in the low green houses in the hills. I'm beginnin' to wonder meself, Bridget, if I *am* the smartest man in Ireland!"

Bridget smiled. "If you've reached that stage in your thinkin', Patrick," she said, "you're halfway already to bein' as smart a man as you think you are."

7

The
Iron
Knife

FIRST PART

When Kieron was properly well again, Patrick gave him the blue stone for himself and told him to keep it by him always, and he stayed close to the house for a while, afraid to let the boy out of his sight for fear something would happen to him. He made whistles for him and a fishing-rod that was just right for his size. And when Kieron asked him where he had got the blue stone, he told him the story of the strange old woman and the present she had given him for his kindness to her.

Indeed, he was never tired of telling the tale of his adventures to Kieron, for the sound of his own voice was sweet music in the ears of Patrick Kentigern Keenan. Nor was Kieron ever tired of listening to him, and on the winter nights when the curtains were drawn and the lamp lit, Patrick would sit in his chair by the fire with Kieron on a stool at his feet. Then he would light his pipe, and when the blue smoke was puffing upwards, he would talk to Kieron, and the boy would fix his big dark eyes on his father's face and listen to every word.

"I wish it would happen to me, Da," he would say at the end of every story. "I wish I could meet with a fairy-man."

Bridget had no patience with this story-telling. "You're filling the boy's head with nonsense," she said, for it made her uneasy to see how Kieron drank in every word that Patrick said.

"Nonsense doesn't get you a pair of new shoes, a golden spoon, a golden necklace, a silver bridle, and a magic stone," Patrick reminded her.

"But you never got the gold in the low green houses in the hills, Da," Kieron said.

"He got something that was worth more, son," said Bridget, "and so did you."

"See you never lose the blue stone, boy," Patrick added. "It took the smartest man in Ireland to win that for you."

"Oh, Patrick!" Bridget sighed. "And here I was after thinkin' you'd forgot that foolish vow."

"I'll forget it when everybody else in Connemara remembers it," said Patrick, "and not before."

Whatever else he was, you had to admit that Patrick Kentigern Keenan was the most stubborn man in Ireland.

"When are you goin' to look for the fairies' gold, Da? When are you?" Kieron asked him, but Patrick wouldn't say. And still the boy kept at it with his questions, till at last Patrick had to say "Never," and tell him not to talk about it any more.

The truth was that in spite of his boasts he was coming to believe that he had tried his luck far enough against the fairies. A man might win against them so often, but there would come a time when his luck would give out, and then——

"And then what?" asked Kieron, when Patrick talked like this one night.

"And then you'll be their bond-slave forever," Patrick told him. "You'll live far underground and never see the upper

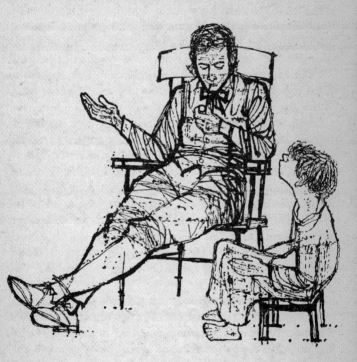

earth again except by moonlight. You'll do the fairies' work for them, tending their cattle, shaping the little pieces of flint they use for arrow-heads, or maybe they'll teach you the cunning ways they have of fashioning gold into chains and brooches. It might be that they'd put you to brewing the heather ale that only they have the secret of making, or maybe they'd teach you to make the poison they use to tip their arrow-heads."

"I would run away," said Kieron.

Patrick shook his head. "There would be nowhere to run to," he said, "for the fairy queen would only have to touch your eyes and you would forget who you were and where you came from, and if your own mother was to walk in at the door and say, 'Kieron, come home,' you wouldn't know her."

"You're frightenin' the boy," said Bridget, and sent him to bed. But Kieron was a brave boy for all his few years. There was no fear in him of fairies or of anything else, and as he lay in his little narrow bed and thought of the fairies' gold, it seemed to him that it would be a greater adventure than ever his father had had if he could go in search of it.

One night, when he had been thinking like this before he went to sleep, he woke up and found the room filled with moonlight. He sat up in bed, and a great longing came on him to go out into the moonlight and search for the fairies' gold. He got out of bed and very quietly put on his clothes and went to the door. He opened it a crack, and listened. Faintly in the distance, he heard voices calling, *"Kieron! Kieron! Kieron Keenan!"*

The voices sang his name as if it were the words of a song and without a word spoken to tell him, Kieron knew that if he followed the voices they would lead him to the fairy-houses in the hills. "And to the fairies' gold," he whispered, and ran out across the moonlit grass.

When Patrick and Bridget woke up the next morning and found that Kieron was not in the house, they looked for him in the fields around. But he was not to be seen, and with fear growing on them, they searched the countryside high and low, but there was not a trace of the boy to be found.

"He's fallen into a bog," cried Bridget.

"Not him," Patrick said. "He's sure-footed as a goat." He

went out to the shed and got out the broken blade of a plough-share. Then he made a fireplace of stones, built a fire in it, and thrust the blade into the heart of the fire. Bridget followed and watched him.

"There's only one place he can have gone," Patrick said, looking up at her. "Him with all his questions about the fairies' gold and how to find the fairy-houses. He's gone to look for the fairies' gold."

"It was you stuffed his head with all these tales," sobbed Bridget. "We'll never get him back now."

Patrick rose to his feet. "There is one way, and one way only to save the boy," he said. "So listen to me, Bridget, for this is the sober truth I'm tellin' you."

Bridget dabbed at her eyes with her apron, and Patrick went on, "There's no mortal man can enter a fairy-house and come out again at his own free will and pleasure, for the door of it will shut fast behind him the moment he steps inside it, and none but the fairies have the power to open it again. And so he is trapped. But if a man takes with him a knife that is made, blade and hilt, of iron, and if he sticks that iron knife into the doorpost of the fairy-house before he enters it, the door cannot close behind him. For iron is the one thing the fairies have no power over, and it is the one thing that they fear."

"And is that an iron knife you're makin'?" asked Bridget, and Patrick said grimly, "It is."

"It will be a dangerous thing to do," she whispered. Patrick said nothing, and Bridget looked from the iron heating in the fire to his face, and she saw that he was afraid of the thing he had to do. And she loved him because he meant to save Kieron, even though he was afraid.

The day was nearly gone before the iron knife was made, and when it was ready, Patrick stuck it into his belt. Then he put the golden spoon, the golden necklace, and the silver bridle into the pockets of his coat. He put on the leprechaun's shoes and took the parcel of bread and cheese that Bridget had made for him. He was ready to go. But before he left, he put his hands on Bridget's shoulders and looked down into her face.

"I'll find Kieron," he said. "I'll bring him back, Bridget. I promise you."

"I believe you," she said. "But hurry, Patrick, hurry."

And so Patrick set out for the hills. "This time," he said as he tramped along, "it's them or me." And he gripped hard on the iron hilt of the iron knife, for well he knew that if Kieron was a prisoner of the fairies it would be a fight to the death to save him.

The last of the daylight faded away, and as darkness fell, the rain began to come down in big, heavy drops. The rain got heavier till it was a solid downpour, and Patrick had to walk with his head down and his eyes half-shut against the

force of it. Thunder began to roll and crack, and lightning split the sky open with jagged, yellow streaks. The storm was right overhead. The rain soaked him, the thunder deafened him, the lightning blinded him, but the rage burning in his heart was fiercer than the storm. When it was at its height, he stopped and looked upwards, shaking his fist.

"Shake the sky and break the sky!" he shouted. "You'll not stop me comin' for my Kieron."

Then he bent to his walk again, his long legs covering the ground in swift, strong strides. After a while, the storm died away and the moon floated in and out among the cloud wrack. The air was very still and silent after the storm, so still that Patrick jumped when he heard his name called. He stood still and listened, and heard it again.

"*Patrick Kentigern Keenan,*" a high sweet voice was calling, with a wild singing sound on the "*Ke-e-e-nan.*" The voice was on the left of him and he turned toward it, but another voice on his right took up the cry, singing his name on that high, sweet note. A voice called from in front of him, another sang behind him; then from all sides the sweet, shrill voices took up the wild singing of his name.

Patrick stopped, cold shivers of fear running down his back. Something touched his cheek—something that felt like the touch of a soft, cold hand—and behind him a voice laughed. He whirled round. There was nothing there, but behind him now he felt a warm breath on his neck and in his ear a voice whispered, "*Patrick Kentigern Keenan.*"

Patrick's heart began to thump wildly. "Easy now, easy," he muttered to himself. He set his teeth, turned, and walked deliberately on the way he had been going. More voices sounded behind him, whispering and laughing. His foot caught on a long tussock of grass and he fell headlong. He struggled to his feet and felt his hair being pulled by invisible hands, and at that he gave a roar of rage.

"Leave your hands off me whoever you are," he shouted, "or I'll swipe you where you stand even though ye're not there."

He listened for a minute, but there was no sound except the rustling of the grass at his feet. Patrick drew a deep breath of relief. "Now I *know* I'm the bravest man in Ireland," he said, and he walked on—a lean, lonely figure trudging through the darkness of the hills. Maybe he was not so brave as he thought he was, but he was a brave man all the same.

He began to whistle as he walked, to keep his spirits up, and after a while he noticed a strange thing. He was whistling a tune he had never heard before. Did I make that up in my head? he wondered, and stopped whistling to think about it. But the tune went on, low and soft in the air all round him, the notes as clear and sweet as if they had been rung on fine glass.

Patrick sank down on the grass and listened like a man in a trance, and the strange thing was, the grass beneath him was not long and cold and wet, but the soft, warm, springy grass of early summer. He lay back on the soft cushion it made and the music drifted all about him. He closed his eyes and smelled the sharp, sweet smell of thyme and knew that if he opened his eyes again he would see bluebells waving in the grass beside his head. The sun would be darting long golden rays down out of the blue sky and there would be the brown speck of a lark singing high above him as he lay there.

It was all there in the sadness and sweetness of the music, all the feel of the barefoot, golden days he had almost forgotten, when he had lain in the sun a little lad no bigger than his own Kieron—*Kieron!* Patrick's eyes flew open and he jerked upright. The music that had tricked him was still trembling sweetly in the air, but the grass under him was cold and wet, and instead of the warm sunny air of his dream there was only the chilly darkness of the night.

He groaned and shivered as he stumbled to his feet, for he knew now that the music was only another trick of the fairies to stop him coming for Kieron, and this time they had almost succeeded. He put his hands over his ears to shut out the music, but still he heard it in his head and every note of it was a terrible temptation to him to lie down again and dream the sweet dreams of his boyhood's summer. He stopped walking and glared all about him.

"Save yer breath to cool yer porridge," he shouted. "Ye'll not stop me comin' for my Kieron."

He began to sing to drown out the sound of the music, marching along and roaring out at the top of his voice every song that he could remember and a few more that he made up as he went along. He may not have had the best voice in Ireland, but there was no doubt about it that he had the loudest, and when he stopped at last as much for want of breath as because there wasn't a song left in his head, the fairy music was no longer to be heard.

"Now, if that isn't a blessed silence," said Patrick. And indeed it was, for the noise he had been making could have been heard over three counties. The first finger of dawn was in the sky, and as the sun came up, he sat down to eat his bread and cheese. Then he had a drink from a stream that ran with dark peaty water and stood up, wiping his mouth with the back of his hand and considering which way he should go.

Ahead of him he could see a track that led westward and it seemed to him to be the same path he had followed with the old woman who had given him the blue stone. "That's the road for me," said Patrick, and he set off along it, gazing ahead for the circle of thorn bushes where the old woman had disappeared. Toward noon he saw them, and his heart beat like a drum as he came up to the edge of them and saw a big, low green mound in the center of the thicket.

The thorn bushes were old, with knotty, twisted stems that crouched low to the ground and there was no path through them, but Patrick had not braved the storm and the calling voices and the fairy music to be beaten by some thorn bushes in the end. He drew the iron knife from his belt, plunged forward, and began to hack a path for himself through the thicket.

It was no easy job. The noonday sun beat down on his head so that the sweat ran into his eyes and blinded him.

Sharp though the iron knife was, the thick stems turned the blade, branches whipped back against his face, and long, pointed thorns tore at his hands. But Patrick Kentigern Keenan was a strong man and an angry man, and he wielded the knife like a sword. And because he had forged the blade straight and true and because the knife, blade and hilt, was of iron, it cut a way for him through the thicket of fairy thorn.

When he was up to the mound at last, he saw a door set in its side. It was colored like the grass and roots around and set so cunningly in place that he had to look closely before he could see where it was. There was a handle to it like a gnarled piece of root growing out of the grass. Patrick put his hand to it; then he hesitated. What lay behind that door? Did someone lie in wait for him? Would a shower of poisoned arrows fall on him as he opened it? "Well, I'm not the bravest man in Ireland for nothing," he muttered between his teeth, and pulled at the door.

It opened slowly, heavily, under his hand, with a whisper of grass and a rustle of leaves as it swung back against the side of the mound. Patrick crouched waiting, with the knife in his hand. No sound or movement came from within the door. Slowly he straightened up. He raised his arm to his

shoulder and with all his strength thrust the iron knife into the doorpost.

"I'm coming, Kieron," Patrick said softly, and stepped through the doorway.

8
The
Iron
Knife

SECOND PART

In the dim light that came through the open doorway, Patrick stretched out his arms and felt a stone wall on either side of him. He was in a passage. The ground sloped downwards under his feet, and with his hands guiding him on either side, he walked down the sloping passage. The daylight from the open door lasted only a few yards and then he was walking blind, never knowing what might leap at him out of the darkness.

After a while the floor of the passage leveled out, and at the end of the level bit of passage he could see light coming through an arched doorway. He crept toward the arch, shaking in every limb with fear, but when he reached it he stood there with his eyes open and his mouth open and his fear quite forgotten with the wonder of what he saw.

The doorway was the entrance to a great hall with walls lined with stone and a stone floor covered with green rushes. It was lit by gleaming gold lamps that hung by chains from the high roof, and at the far end of the hall seated on a golden throne that stood on a raised step, there was a woman with a golden crown on her head.

The hall was filled with people, small creatures about as high as a tall man's waist, all dressed in green the color of new grass. The men had green hoods that finished in a point at the top, and the women had long hair floating round their shoulders. This long hair streaming down made the young women look very beautiful, but the old women that were there looked evil and witchlike with their gray hair tangled on their shoulders and falling raggedly over their wizened faces.

All the faces were turned toward Patrick. There was not a sound in the great hall as they stared at him. He knew that he had to make a move and he began to walk down the length of the hall toward the throne. His knees were shaking under him, but he held himself tall and straight so that his step grew steady. And so Patrick Kentigern Keenan kept his dignity as he came from the upper earth to seek for his son among the fairies.

It seemed a long way to walk in silence. The fairy people stood back to let him pass, and he saw that there was a great dog lying across the step at the foot of the fairy queen's throne. It was as black as coal with ears laid flat back against its head and small eyes that gleamed red and wicked. Patrick kept his eyes fixed on it for he could see the fur lifting on its back and he heard the growl growing in its throat. He was halfway down the hall when the dog rose to its feet. Patrick's hand stole into his pocket, but he kept on walking. The fairy queen bent and whispered to the dog; then she leaned back in her seat and laughed as the beast hurled itself forward.

It came at Patrick like a black thunderbolt. He drew his hand out of his pocket and crouched, waiting for it, with the golden necklace dangling from his fingers. It leaped for his throat, its jaws wide open, red and snarling. Patrick was borne over backwards by its weight, but as he fell managed to slip the golden chain over its head, and then he lay there with his eyes shut waiting for the dog to savage him.

"If it's ate alive I'm goin' to be," he said to himself, "I'd rather not see it happen."

But nothing happened, and Patrick cautiously opened one eye. The dog was standing beside him with its head hanging and its tail between its legs. It looked as meek as a mouse. Patrick scrambled to his feet. "Come on, ye ugly brute that ye are," he said, and twisted his fingers in the golden chain that hung round its neck.

He marched up to the fairy queen dragging the black dog behind him, and bowed to her, holding his hat against his chest as he knew was the polite thing to do. "I'm returnin' your dog, ma'am," he said, "for I haven't much use for a big soft creature the like of him."

"How did you know," said the fairy queen, "that the golden necklace would tame him?"

"I didn't, as ye 'might say, *know*," Patrick said cheerfully. "My way of reasonin' was that a golden chain that turned a strong courageous man like myself into a hare might well turn your hound into something entirely unlike his natural self. And I was right, ye see, though that's small wonder since I happen to be the smartest man in Ireland."

"Then," said the fairy queen, "you must be Patrick Kentigern Keenan."

"The same, ma'am," Patrick said, and he gave another elegant bow. He straightened up and looked her in the eye. "I've come to fetch my son Kieron," he said, and his voice was as harsh and hard as iron grating against rock.

But the fairy queen pretended not to notice the change in his voice. "What am I thinking of!" she exclaimed. "Here is a visitor come to see us and I have not offered him a thing to eat after his long journey." She clapped her hands and called, "Bring a bowl of broth for Mister Keenan;" then she turned and smiled at Patrick, and he was very much afraid of her. She was very beautiful. Her hair was black and long and shining. Her eyes were as green as a shallow sea. Her skin was as white and pure as a white rose, but the smile on her rose-red mouth was like a candle lighting up all the evil thoughts in her head.

A fairy-woman came and put a small bowl full of steaming broth into his hand. There was a strange smell from it, a smell that Patrick knew, and it was the smell of the poison berries that Kieron had eaten on the night he nearly died.

"You that knows so much," the fairy queen said softly, "you must know that only one with greater power than myself can take Kieron from me. Drink the broth, Patrick, and see if your power is greater than mine."

"I'll drink it," Patrick said grimly. He drew the golden spoon from his pocket. "I'll sup with your own spoon," he said, "that was given and taken in kindness." He dipped the spoon in the bowl, but the fairy queen jumped up with a cry of rage and struck bowl and spoon from his hands. "Well you know that no harm can come to one that sups from that spoon," she shouted.

"Indeed and I didn't know till this minute," Patrick said thankfully, "but it's glad I am to know that's the case."

"And sorry you'll be that you ever set foot here," the fairy queen said, her face all twisted with rage. She clapped her hands again and the fairy-men and women standing all round them scattered in panic. Patrick looked round to see the cause of it and he had not far to look. A group of fairy-men had appeared, goading a white bull in front of them with pointed sticks. Now they dropped the sticks and scattered for safety, and Patrick was left alone in the middle of the clear space facing the bull and wishing he had never been born.

The bull's head was down. It pawed the ground and snorted and tossed its head wildly. The lamplight gleamed on its polished black hoofs and glinted off the long white horns. It was a beautiful creature and the fiercest thing Patrick had ever seen in his life. He gave one yell and turned and ran with the bull after him. The next thing he knew, he had tripped and lay flat on the ground, and the bull's horns were flashing down at him. He rolled aside in the nick of time, the bull's horns struck the place where he had been and he was on his feet again, dodging and twisting and turning with the bull bearing down on him all the time like a white fury.

The horns flashed along the sleeve of his jacket and tore his coattails to ribbons. Once he got in a smack at its nose with his closed fist, but the bellow it gave turned his stomach right over with fear. "I shouldn't have done that," he panted. "Sure, I don't know my own strength—I might have killed the beast." Then he turned and ran for his life again, and all the time he ran he was feeling in his pocket for the silver bridle. He got it out at last, and the jingle of the silver bells was the sweetest music he had ever heard.

The bull was coming up on him at the charge, but with the bridle in his hand Patrick held his ground. It thundered at him, head down, and as its head swung up and the horns struck out to gore him, Patrick stepped nimbly to one side and swung the silver bridle over the bull's head. The speed of its charge carried it past him. It slithered to a stop and stood there panting, all the rage and fierceness draining out of it at the magic touch of the fairy bridle. Patrick was up on it in a couple of bounds. A twist and a pull, and he had the bit in its mouth and the reins gathered into his hands. Then he laid hold on its horns and swung himself onto its back.

"Get on there," Patrick said. He kicked his heels into the bull's sides, and as meek and tame now as any well-bred saddle-horse it trotted with Patrick on its back up to the fairy queen's throne. "I'm sorry, indeed, ma'am," he said, sliding to the ground, "that it took so long to bridle the creature for you. It's fast on its feet, as you can see, and took a while for me to catch." And he grinned to himself, thinking to see the anger on her face at being beaten for the third time.

But the fairy queen only smiled. "You are a proper man, Patrick Kentigern Keenan," she said. "You have courage and cunning and laughter in you." She bent close to him. "Come and live with us, Patrick," she said softly. Patrick looked away, afraid to meet the shallow, sea-green of her eyes and he tried to shut his ears to what she was saying, but he heard her in spite of himself. "You will go finely clad, Patrick," she said, "and there will be golden rings on your fingers and you will hunt with swift white hounds on scarlet leashes. You will drink the heather ale and it will be fiery sweet on your tongue, and you will dance in the moonlight with your heels as light as feathers and you leaping so that you could touch the moon with the tips of your fingers. There will always be music in your ears, Patrick—the music of high summer with larks singing and the warm wind piping in the soft, dry grass. Only go in bondage to me, Patrick, and you will have the freedom of all Ireland and be a power in the land. Only go in bondage to me, Patrick, only to me."

And Patrick would not meet her eyes though he longed with all his heart to look at her, for if he did he would be face to face with the thing he had dreaded when he set his hand to the latch of the door in the mound above. She would look him through and through with her sea-green eyes and she would spare his life and steal from him his immortal soul. And Kieron would never go free.

"The boy, ma'am," he said hoarsely, and kept his eyes fixed on her small green shoes peeping out from under the fine white stuff of her gown. "Where is the boy?"

There was a long silence. One half of Patrick's heart was heavy with sorrow for all the fine delights she had promised and he would never see, and the other half was light and proud with courage that he had passed the last test of her power.

"Bring the boy," the fairy queen said.

Patrick looked up at her. Her face was stern and cold and cruel. Patrick began to tremble. He looked all round him and the fairy-men and women looked silently back at him with stern, cold looks. They parted their ranks, and a little boy came out between them and came up to where Patrick stood before the queen's throne.

"Kieron," Patrick cried. The boy looked at him. He was the same age as Kieron. He wore Kieron's clothes, and his face was Kieron's face. "Come away home with me, Kieron," Patrick begged, but the boy only looked at him with eyes that were dead and cold and gave no look or sign that he had heard Patrick or knew who he was.

"Take your son, Patrick," said the fairy queen.

"I want to stay with you," the boy cried. He stretched out his hands to her and looked at Patrick with his dead, cold eyes. "Why should I go with you? I do not know you," he said. He turned again to the fairy queen, and she laughed loud and long, and all the fairy-men and women standing round them laughed with her.

The loud, cruel laughter swelled all round Patrick, and a terrible rage grew in him. "Put your hand in your breeches pocket," he said to the boy, and wondering, the boy obeyed him. "Now draw out what is there and give it to me," said Patrick, and the boy drew out his hand and put into Patrick's hand the round stone of a curious dull blue color that he had got from the old woman.

He bent over the boy. "Kieron Keenan," he said, "be healed of the spell the fairies have put upon your sight," and lightly touched both his eyes with the blue stone as he spoke. The boy blinked once or twice. He rubbed his eyes and stared at Patrick. Tears grew up in his eyes and spilled

over like drops of broken crystal onto his cheeks. "Da!" he
said. "It's yourself, Da." He rushed into Patrick's open arms.
"Take me home, Da," he wept. "Take me home."

Patrick looked over his head to the fairy queen. Her face
was stony hard. "All the fairies in Connemara are in this
hall," she said. "All the magic in Connemara is against you,
Patrick." Her rose-red mouth smiled a small, secret smile,
and her green eyes glittered in the light of the golden lamps.
"Take the boy," she said, "and go from here. *If you can.*"

"Good day to you then, ma'am," Patrick said, polite to the
last. He turned, and with Kieron in his arms started walking
toward the arch through which he had come.

The fairy-men and women parted to let him through, and
Kieron hid his face against his father's shoulder at their angry
looks. If they guess about the iron knife in the doorpost, we're
done for, Patrick thought, and clutched Kieron tighter. The
fairy people closed in behind him and followed as he entered
the passage. He did not look round as he heard their steps
behind him in the darkness, but it took him all his courage
not to break into a run.

The passage began to slope upwards and Patrick lengthened his stride. The darkness turned to a dim gray that grew
lighter as he went on. The fairies behind him began to mut-
ter. "Run, Da, run," Kieron whispered. The muttering rose
to a shout of rage as the fairies saw the dim light growing to
daylight from the open door. "Run," Kieron shrieked, but
Patrick was already running, his long legs taking one stride
to every three of the fairy-men's short ones.

He bounded up the last few steps of the passage and
through the open door. He dropped Kieron, snatched the
knife from the doorpost, and pushed the door shut with a
great thud. Then, just as the first wave of fairy-men surged
against it, he drew back his arm and with all his force thrust
the iron knife into the center of the wood.

"There's one thing you have no power over," he shouted. "You'll never open that door while the iron knife is there."

A scream of rage from many voices came from behind the door. The note of the scream rose higher and higher. It grew louder and the sound of it echoed over the quiet hillside. The echo came back to them with a shrill, piercing sweetness and it seemed to Patrick that all the voices now were blended into one voice that was calling to him, and this voice had a great sweetness in it and a sadness such as he had never heard before.

He crouched, listening, among the thorn trees and felt his heart would break with the strange, sad beauty of the sound. Like a man in a dream, he rose to his feet and put his hand to the iron knife to pluck it from the door, but Kieron jumped up and hung onto his arm with all his strength.

"Leave the knife, Da," he shouted. "Remember her face! Remember her eyes!"

Patrick looked down at him. Kieron's face was wild with fear. "Her eyes?" Patrick asked. He thought of the fairy queen's eyes, green eyes, green as a shallow sea, and he remembered the way they had glittered when she said, "Go from here. *If you can.*" He shivered, and his hand dropped from the iron knife. "Let us go home, boy," he said.

He turned his back on the fairy mound and led Kieron through the thorn trees, and they set off for home with the wild, lost sweetness of the fairy queen's voice ringing in their ears. Behind him Patrick had left the golden spoon, the golden necklace, and the silver bridle. Even the blue stone lay forgotten where it had dropped to the floor when the spell on Kieron's sight was broken. He clasped Kieron's hand tightly in his. "I have lost most everything I had from the fairies," he said, "but I have got my son Kieron safely home again."

Not another word did Patrick speak till he got home, and

Kieron had nothing to say either for he was so tired that
Patrick carried him in his arms most of the way and he fell
asleep against his father's shoulder. Bridget came running to
meet them, laughing and crying in the one breath as she took
the sleepy boy in her arms, and they all went in together to
the supper she had ready for them.

"Now, Patrick," she said, "tell me everything that has
happened."

And so Patrick told her the whole story of Kieron's rescue from the fairies, with every word that had passed between himself and the fairy queen. And except that the black dog and the white bull grew a bit in the telling, it was more or less a true account of his adventures.

Bridget sat spellbound with Kieron on her lap till he had finished, and with a look at the boy and a sigh as she said it, she asked:

"So the golden spoon has gone?"

"It has," said Patrick, "and the silver bridle and the blue stone, too."

"And the golden necklace?" she asked mournfully.

"Everything I ever had from the fairies is gone," said Patrick, "everything except for my new shoes."

"They were the beginning of all your trouble." Bridget sighed. "We're all peaceful and happy now, Patrick, and so we'll always be if you give up this foolish notion that you're the smartest man in Ireland."

"Never!" shouted Patrick, "for now I have the proof of it. Wasn't I after tellin' you there's not a fairy can get out of that mound while the iron knife is in the door?"

"They're locked up forever?" asked Bridget.

"All the fairies in Connemara," Patrick said triumphantly, "locked up forever behind the door with the iron knife in it."

Bridget began to smile. "Well, I do believe——" she began.

"And you're not the only one," Patrick cried. "There's more than you will see that it took a smart man to do *that!*"

Trust Patrick for it, the whole countryside soon knew the story of the iron knife, but telling the tale was one thing and getting them to believe it was another. Everyone remembered the story of the new shoes, and it was whispered that this was just a yarn that Patrick was putting about to get even with them for the laugh they had had over the way the leprechaun had tricked him.

It was not long though before people began to say that when the wind was in a certain quarter they could hear a strange, sweet voice calling at night from the hills. There were others who laughed at this for so much nonsense, and one night a party of men led by Mulhoy the cattle-dealer set out to follow the path that Patrick said he had taken to the fairy mound.

"For," said Mulhoy, "sure, we'll prove this story of an iron knife is only another taradiddle of Keenan's—like the hundred head of fairy cattle he had to sell me and what had he but a cloud of flies."

But Mulhoy and his men came back in the morning, white and shaken, and admitted that they had seen the iron knife in the door of the mound, and heard loud knocking and voices calling and lamenting from under the earth.

"Keenan," said Mulhoy, "I take back all that I said."

"Be easy, Mulhoy," Patrick said grandly. "Sure, ye knew no better, man."

"No, indeed," Mulhoy said humbly. "Ah, but it's a smart man you are, Keenan."

Patrick looked at Bridget, and she smiled proudly back at him. It was his moment of triumph, and he rose to the occasion like the great man he had always known himself to be. He looked down at his feet in the leprechaun's new shoes. Everybody followed his look, and there was not a smile among them. He planted his feet well apart, tipped his hat jauntily over one eye, and put his hands on his hips. And standing like that, he looked up and grinned at all the folk around him waiting solemnly to hear what he would say next.

"Smart, did ye say, Mulhoy? I'm the smartest man in Ireland!" said Patrick Kentigern Keenan.

And this time, everybody believed him.